Ma Lien and the Magic Brush

By HISAKO KIMISHIMA

English version by ALVIN TRESSELT

Illustrated by KEI WAKANA

This book translated from *Ma Lien To Maho No Fude* originally published by Kaisei Sha, Tokyo, Japan.

PARENTS' MAGAZINE PRESS · NEW YORK

There once lived in China a poor peasant boy named Ma Lien.
Day after day he worked hard in the fields
so that he would have food to eat and a small hut to live in.
Ma Lien's greatest dream was to be an artist,
but the boy had not so much as a copper coin
with which to buy a brush.
One day as he trudged along under a heavy load,
he passed by the house of a famous artist.
Going over to the gate in the high wall, Ma Lien peeked in,
hoping to see the great man at work.

Silently he stood, watching the artist
as he painted a portrait of the mandarin.
At last the boy could hold his excitement
no longer, and he boldly spoke up.
"Oh, great one," he said, "could you let me have
one of your brushes—an old one that you don't need
anymore—so that I, too, might paint a picture?"
On hearing this unexpected voice the artist turned around.
When he saw it was only a poor peasant boy daring to ask
for one of his brushes he became very angry.
"Ha, so you think you would like to paint!" he cried.
"Away with you and back to your fields!"
And he drove the frightened Ma Lien from his gate.

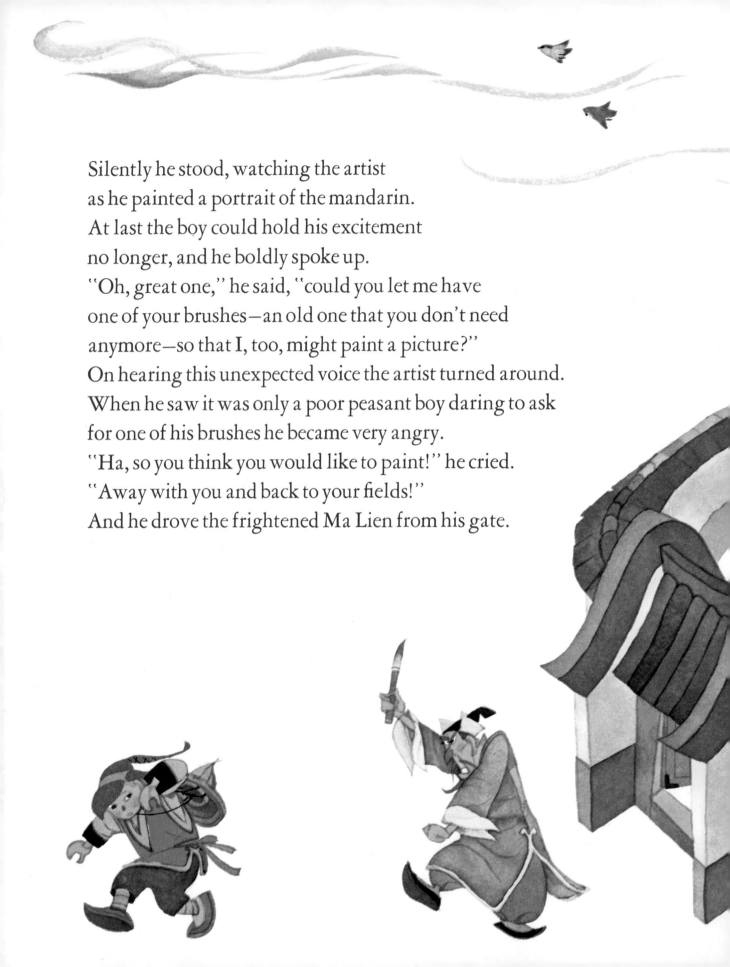

But Ma Lien would not be discouraged. He drew pictures wherever he could, using a stone to scratch on a flat rock, or his fingers to draw in the wet sand of the riverbank.

When he went back to his hut at night, he drew pictures on the wall by the light of a flickering candle. Soon he had covered the walls with pictures of everything he could think of.

With practice, Ma Lien became
more and more skillful.
One day he drew a picture
of a small chicken. A hawk flew by
and circled around and around,
thinking it was a real chicken.
Another time he drew a scowling wolf
on a rock in the pasture.
The cows and sheep were so frightened
by this wolf that they would not
go near the rock, even though it was
surrounded with lush sweet grass.

But with all his skill, Ma Lien still did not
have a brush. Lying one night on his bed
he looked around his room at all the pictures
he had scratched on the clay walls and sighed.
"Oh, if only I had a brush," he said.
"What beautiful pictures I would paint."
With that there was a flash of light,
and standing before the boy was an old wizard.
He was leaning on a twisted cane,
and his white beard fell to the floor.
"Ma Lien," he said in a creaky voice,
    "You have worked very hard
    and now you have earned a brush.
    Use it wisely,
    for it has great power."
    And saying this he handed
    the trembling boy
    a beautiful paintbrush.
    Before Ma Lien could even
    stammer out a thank you,
    the old man had vanished.

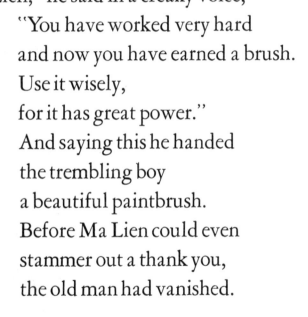

With a cry of joy the boy rushed over
to the one bare spot on his wall
and quickly painted a proud and happy rooster.
But he had no sooner painted the last curling feather
of the rooster's tail when the bird sprang from the wall
and flew to the windowsill. There he gave
a great *cock-a-doodle-doo* and disappeared
into the night. "Now I know why the wizard
said this brush had great power," said Ma Lien.
"Do not worry, old man. I *will* use it wisely."

The next morning as Ma Lien was walking
to the mountain to gather firewood, he passed
a rice paddy. There he saw a man and a young boy
pulling a heavy plow to till the paddy. Ma Lien
quickly went over to the wall of an old shed
and painted a strong and healthy water buffalo.
Again, just as he finished, the beast leaped
from the wall and with a low *moooo* he lumbered down
to the paddy. Now with the help of the buffalo
the man and his son soon had the paddy
ready for planting.

Just at that moment the mandarin
came by, and seeing the power
of Ma Lien's magic brush, he ordered
his men to seize the poor boy.

When they had brought Ma Lien to the mandarin, he commanded the boy to paint a pile of silver coins for him. Ma Lien, remembering the wizard's words, refused, and the mandarin had him thrown in the dungeon with his other prisoners.

Ma Lien soon discovered that the other men had done
no wrong, but had been imprisoned by the mandarin
so that he could steal their lands. "Never fear,"
said the boy, "I will have us all free before too long."
As the night passed, Ma Lien waited until the guards
had dozed off. Then quickly he painted a door on the wall.
The prisoners pushed against it, the door swung open and they
fled into the night. The mandarin's men came chasing
after Ma Lien, but the boy easily escaped on the fine horse
he had painted for himself.

Ma Lien knew he would not be safe if he remained
on the mandarin's lands, so he rode for many miles
until he came to a strange village. Here he continued
to help anyone he could with his magic brush.
He painted buffaloes to help the farmers in their fields.
He painted chickens for the farmers' wives,
and he painted toys to keep the children happy.
One day he came upon some farmers hard at work
carrying buckets of water to their
dried-up fields. "That work is
much too hard for you," said Ma Lien,
and he set about painting a fine
water wheel so that it would be easier
to bring the water from the river
into the fields. And so it was
that Ma Lien and his wonderful brush
became known throughout the land.

It wasn't long before the mandarin
learned where Ma Lien was living.
He sent his soldiers to the village
and when they found the boy
they seized him and dragged him
back to the palace.

The mandarin instantly took away the brush
and commanded that the boy be thrown
into the dungeon. "Without this I don't
think he will escape so easily," he laughed.
Then he sent for the court painter
and ordered him to paint a picture
with the brush.
"What would you have me paint?" he asked.
"A tree," said the mandarin. "A tree
with leaves of gold that will fall
like the rain when I shake the branches."

The artist went right to work and soon had a fine tree painted on the wall of the palace. But when the mandarin rushed to shake the tree he got no more than a bump on the head for his trouble. The tree was nothing but a painting on the wall.

Now the mandarin realized that only Ma Lien
could paint pictures that would become real.
Sending for the boy, he spoke kindly to him.
"Ma Lien," he said softly, "if you will paint
but one picture for me I will give you your freedom."
The boy, thinking of a way to trick the greedy man,
agreed to do as he was asked.

The mandarin's eyes lit up with delight. He handed the
brush to Ma Lien and said, "Paint me a mountain of pure gold."
The boy went to work at once, painting a broad expanse
of blue sea. The wide sea spread all across the wall.
"Why do you paint the sea?" demanded the mandarin.
"I ordered a mountain of gold."
"I have not finished," said the boy quietly, and with that
he painted a great gold mountain rising up out of the sea.
"Beautiful, beautiful!" cried the man.
"Now paint me a ship so that I can sail
to my mountain and bring back the gold."

In a twinkling Ma Lien had
painted a fine ship, worthy
of a mandarin who was about
to travel to a mountain of gold.
The man wasted no time in hurrying
aboard with a troop of his finest
soldiers. The sail was raised
and slowly the ship rode out
to sea.

"Too slow, too slow!" shouted
the mandarin. "Give us a wind
to speed us along." Obediently,
Ma Lien painted a wind cloud.
The wind came whistling down
and the sails filled out. The wind
ruffled the water and great waves
rose about the ship.

"Too much!" cried the mandarin angrily. "You will sink my ship." But Ma Lien payed no attention. He went right on painting storm clouds. Now the wind howled and shrieked, and the waves crashed about the ship. Then with a great *crrrack*, the ship split in two and sank in the stormy waters.

Once more Ma Lien returned to his simple life with the peasants, always ready to help them with their work. And never again was he forced to use his magic brush for evil and greed.